Ha
V
H

Ge

Pl
Yo
O

the year 776 BC, the first
ic Games were held in a town
Olympia in Ancient Greece.
years later, a boy named Olly
up there, dreaming of being
Olympic champion. But first,
uld have to be better than his
arch-enemy, Spiro...

ORCHARD BOOKS
338 Euston Road, London NW1 3BH
Orchard Books Australia
Level 17/207 Kent Street, Sydney, NSW 2000

First published in 2011
First paperback publication in 2012

ISBN 978 1 40831 184 4 (hardback)
ISBN 978 1 40831 192 9 (paperback)

Text and illustrations © Shoo Rayner 2011

A CIP catalogue record for this book is available
from the British Library.

1 3 5 7 9 10 8 6 4 2 (hardback)
1 3 5 7 9 10 8 6 4 2 (paperback)

Printed in Great Britain

Orchard Books is a division of Hachette Children's Books,
an Hachette UK company.

www.hachette.co.uk

OLYMPIA

RACE FOR THE STARS

SHOO RAYNER

ORCHARD

CHAPTER ONE

Olly gritted his teeth and leaned his chariot into the turn, pulling hard on the horse's reins.

"Out of my way, Ant Brain!" Olly's arch-enemy, Spiro, yelled at him from his own chariot. "I'm coming through!"

"Not if I can help it!" Olly growled.

Olly's horse knew what to do. It had been round the track so many times that it could run the race in its sleep. Panting and champing at the bit, the horse pulled Olly's chariot skidding towards the next corner. Spiro was left behind, choking in the dust.

Olly's dad, Ariston, ran the gymnasium in Olympia, the town where the Olympic Games were held every four years. Olly and Spiro worked at the gym, helping the athletes and learning sporting skills from them as they trained. Olly dreamed of being an Olympic champion one day.

During the past week, Olly and Spiro had been training for the Junior Chariot Race at the hippodrome – the special track that was built for racing.

Today was their final training session. Only one of them would be picked to race.

Olly's sister, Chloe, jumped up and down at the side of the track. "Woohoo! Go for it, Olly!" she screamed. Chloe was so caught up in the excitement of the race, she let go of Kerberos, Spiro's fierce and loyal dog.

Seeing that his master needed help, Kerberos chased after Olly's chariot, howling and barking like the terrible three-headed hound he was named after.

"Ha, ha! I've got you now!" Spiro laughed. "Good boy, Kerby!"

Heading into the next turn, Olly's horse slipped and lost its footing. Its eyes rolled madly and it whinnied in panic. Kerberos was at its heels, snapping and growling.

6

Spiro barged up on the inside.
Clouds of dust billowed into the air.

"Slow down!" Olly yelled. "We're going to crash!"

"You mean you're going to lose!" Spiro bellowed.

Amid the clash of wood and metal, Olly pulled hard on the reins. The terrified, neighing horse couldn't hear his commands over Kerberos's ceaseless barking. The chariot gave way beneath Olly's feet and he felt himself being hurled through the air towards the dusty ground of the hippodrome track.

"*Ooof!*" Olly landed hard on his elbow.

"*Arrgh!*" Spiro howled as he collapsed into the dirt close by. Not stopping to check if he had broken any bones, he launched himself at Olly. "That was your fault, you idiot!" he yelled in Olly's face. "You should have let me go past!"

Kerberos joined in, barking loudly in Olly's ear. Chloe added to the noise, shouting, "Leave Olly alone, you great big bully!"

"The horses are getting away!" Olly pointed with his good arm. The boys were meant to look after the animals at all times.

"Enough!" A woman's voice cut through the noise. It was Lydia, the owner of the chariots.

Now they were in trouble!

CHAPTER TWO

Chloe and the boys untangled
themselves and clambered to their
feet. Olly and Spiro rubbed the
various parts of their bodies that
were starting to ache.

"Well, at least you can still stand up!" Lydia snapped.

"My backside hurts," Spiro grumbled, rubbing his bottom.

"And my arm really aches," Olly groaned, massaging his elbow.

Lydia sighed. "So who's going to ride my chariot in the junior race tomorrow? You need to be fighting fit to win. Now you're both injured, you've spoilt your chances!"

"I wish *I* could race the chariot tomorrow," Chloe sighed.

The boys stared at each other in amazement. Forgetting their aches and pains, they collapsed in fits of laughter. "Ha, ha! Girls can't race chariots!" they hooted in unison.

"They can too!" Chloe stamped her foot. "Artemis drives her chariot across the sky every night, *and* she can hunt and shoot arrows."

"But Artemis is a goddess and you're just a girl," Olly laughed.

"Well, Artemis must have been a girl too – once!" Chloe snapped back. "It's so unfair that girls can't race."

"Chloe's right," said Lydia. "And those are *my* chariots and *my* horses!" she told the boys angrily. "I was relying on one of you to win the Junior Chariot Race for me tomorrow. Now what am I going to do? My reputation is on the line because you silly boys decided to fight each other instead of practising!"

The winner of a chariot race wasn't the driver of the chariot – it was its owner. So because women weren't allowed to take part in sport in Olympia, chariot racing was the only way that Lydia could compete – and she was very serious about it! "Do you know how much time, money and effort I put into racing?" she bellowed.

The boys hung their heads and drew shapes in the sand with their toes.

"Bring those horses over here!"
Lydia yelled at Hektor, her champion
adult charioteer. "And you there!"
she called to a servant. "Bring some
apples!"

Hektor winked at Olly as he
returned with the horses. "You'll have
to fall many more times before you
become a champion charioteer!"
he smiled.

Lydia took a couple of apples from the servant and fed them to the horses. "You did well," she told the animals. "Shame you had such lousy drivers!"

"Can I give them an apple?" Chloe asked. "I love horses."

Olly saw Lydia watching Chloe with interest. Chloe had a natural way with the horses. She spoke to them gently as she fed them. She stroked their forelocks and scratched them behind the ears. The horses responded to her as if they understood and respected her.

"Maybe you are blessed by Artemis…" Lydia muttered, her voice calmer as her temper faded. "Come with me, Chloe. We can keep an eye on the servants and make sure they brush down the horses properly. As for you two—" She glared at Olly and Spiro. "Get out of my sight – now!"

CHAPTER THREE

A little later, it was time for the athletes' lunch. One of Olly and Spiro's jobs at the gym was to lay the tables in the dining room.

"My elbow still aches!" Olly groaned. He could hardly lift the salad bowls onto the tables.

Spiro waddled round the room like a fat duck. "My bum still hurts!" he complained, rubbing his backside.

"Quack! Quack!" Hektor joked, as he and his fellow athletes sat down to eat their meal.

"It's not funny!" Spiro grumbled. "I could have really hurt myself."

"You drive a chariot like a battering ram!" Hektor laughed. "You need more care and skill."

Just then, the room fell silent as Simonedes, the athletes' old, wrinkly history teacher, went to stand behind his lectern and cleared his throat. Everyday at lunchtime, Simonedes would tell the athletes stories about gods and heroes and all the amazing things they got up to. It was Olly's favourite part of the day. He could listen to Simonedes' stories for hours.

"Tonight is the full moon," Simonedes began. "And as the moon rises, so does the goddess Artemis, riding her chariot through the night sky, shooting her silver moonlight arrows across the Earth.

"Artemis is the sister of Apollo, who is an inspiration to all athletes, being a great warrior, a poet and a musician, too."

The athletes raised their cups to a painting on the dining-room wall and saluted the image of a handsome young man. "Here's to the health of Apollo!" they chorused.

"Artemis is also a great athlete – a great hunter and a fine charioteer," Simonedes continued.

Hektor leaped to his feet. "But Artemis is a woman. She could never be as great as Apollo."

Simonedes raised his eyebrows. "I wouldn't be so sure. She is a deadly shot. Don't let her aim a silver arrow at you tonight, Hektor!"

Hektor's face was pale as he sat down again. Simonedes' words had been more than a warning – they sounded like a prophecy! Would Artemis come for him tonight, angry at the words he had just spoken about her?

"It is said that Artemis was once in love with a giant called Orion," Simonedes continued. "He too was a great hunter and they often hunted together. Orion boasted that he could hunt and kill anything that lived.

"Gaia, the mother goddess of the Earth, was angry at Orion for killing so much in the natural world. She sent a scorpion that stung Orion and poisoned him to death.

"Then Gaia turned the scorpion into stars and sent it up to the heavens as a warning to others.

"Artemis was so sad that she asked her father, Zeus, to place Orion in the heavens as well. And that's where you can see him every night as Artemis goes to visit him, driving her silver chariot across the night sky."

Olly looked up at the paintings on the walls. There was Artemis, bold and brave with her bow and silver arrows, riding across the stars.

Simonedes' stories seemed so real. Olly could almost imagine himself driving a chariot across the sky, too...

"Olly! Spiro!" Hektor called the boys over to his table. "You'll have to sleep with the horses tonight. I'm going to a safe place where Artemis can't find me with her silver arrows!"

Normally, the adult charioteers slept outside with the horses, guarding them to make sure no one could harm them the night before a big race. The boys exchanged a worried look. They didn't want Artemis to find them either!

CHAPTER FOUR

"*Brrr!*" Olly shivered as a cold breeze
wafted down from the mountains.
The boys were camping out near the
horses for the night. "The sky is so
clear tonight," Olly said. "You can
see all the stars in the heavens. Look!
There's Orion."

"And there's the moon!" Spiro pointed at the silvery white disc that was just rising behind the distant mountains. "Come on, let's try to get some sleep."

The boys settled down in the hay and wrapped their cloaks tightly around them.

"Oh, I can't sleep," Olly said, a few seconds later. "Look over there. Is that a shadow under that tree? It looks like a bull-headed monster with giant horns and glowing yellow eyes!"

"It's nothing," said Spiro, nervously. Kerberos growled.

"Good boy, Kerby," Spiro whispered. "You stay on guard and bark if you see anything."

The moon shone down, lighting up the paddocks where the chariot horses were stabled. Insects buzzed loudly in the trees. The leaves rustled in the breeze. Horses whinnied and stamped their feet, agitated by the mysterious sounds of the night.

The boys stayed awake for ages, listening to every strange noise, imagining evil things all around them in the dark pools of moonlight shadows.

Then, unable to keep their eyes open any longer, they fell into a deep sleep and had restless dreams about the creatures from Simonedes' stories.

A noise woke Olly. It sounded like a chariot driving away, but surely that was impossible? Olly knew that Kerberos would bark his head off if anyone tried to steal the horses.

Olly shook his head, blinked and looked around him. He couldn't believe what he saw. "Wake up, Spiro!" he hissed. "One of the horses and a chariot have gone!"

Spiro sprang to his feet. "Get 'em Kerby!" But Kerberos wasn't there. "What the...?"

In the distance, the moonlight picked out a silvery chariot riding through a cloud of ghostly, pale white dust. Without doubt, the driver was a woman! Her long hair and cloak billowed out behind her. The chariot disappeared into the shadows.

"Artemis!" Olly gasped. "It looked like she had Chloe and Kerberos with her too! Come on! Let's go after them."

The boys' bodies still ached from the previous day's crash, but the excitement of the midnight chase made them forget their pain.

"They're heading towards the hippodrome," Spiro hissed, as they ran quietly down the path.

Olly and Spiro sped through the night. The familiar surroundings seemed quite alien in the moonlight. They could hardly believe their eyes when they climbed the ridge of the spectators' embankment and stared down at the hippodrome...

CHAPTER FIVE

Chloe was racing the chariot hard around the course, reaching out towards her horse, talking to it with quiet, encouraging words. The boys always screamed at their horses when they raced.

"Kerby!" Spiro squeaked in a
surprised voice.

Kerberos was in the chariot too!
He was leaning out of the cockpit, a
toothy smile spread across his face.

"Really lean into the turn at the end," a voice called from the other side of the track. Lydia was giving Chloe instructions. It wasn't Artemis after all!

Now Olly understood why the horse had gone so quietly and why Kerberos hadn't barked. Chloe could make them do anything.

Olly and Spiro stared at each other, dumbstruck.

Round and round the course went Chloe. With each turn, Olly's admiration for his sister grew. He had to admit that she was a natural. Chloe seemed to understand the horse and was able to make it follow her commands with ease.

"She can really race that thing!" said Olly. "Look at the way she shifts her weight to keep the chariot stable on the corners."

"Kerby's doing a great job, too!" Spiro said proudly.

Kerberos seemed to be adding his weight, allowing Chloe to take the corners more sharply, cutting vital seconds off each turn.

Lydia strode onto the course and held her hand up. Chloe pulled hard on the reins and drew the chariot to a halt.

Lydia turned to the boys. "Come down here, you two!" she ordered.

Olly hadn't realised that she'd spotted them.

"I think I've found my new junior champion!" she smiled, as the boys made their way onto the track.

The boys looked at each other. "But...she's a girl!" they chorused.

Lydia glared at them. "There's nothing wrong with that! I make the rules round here – and I don't like losing!"

Olly and Spiro crumbled under her withering stare. All their aches and pains returned as Lydia gave them their instructions.

"Take the chariot back to the paddock and get these horses brushed down and rested. Chloe, you come with me. You need some rest before the race in the morning."

"Thanks, Lydia!" Chloe beamed.

"But—" Olly began.

"But what?" Lydia snapped back.

"But…Chloe can't enter the Junior Chariot Race. They won't let her."

Lydia arched an eyebrow. She spoke slowly and clearly so that everyone understood: "*No one argues with me!*"

CHAPTER SIX
᠎᠎᠎᠎᠎᠎᠎᠎᠎᠎᠎᠎᠎

The next day, no one said a word as Chloe climbed into her chariot at the start of the race. No one complained that she was a girl. No one argued with Lydia!

There were five other chariots in the race, each one driven by a hulking boy. They all sneered at Chloe. She was just a girl! Chloe sneered back. She wasn't scared of anyone.

The judge called the chariots to the starting line. "Ten times round the track, and may the best man win!" he instructed.

"Or the best woman!" Lydia yelled across the course.

The judge dropped his hands and shouted, "Go!"

They were off!

Chloe burst into action, battling to get the inside lane. The two sides of the track were separated by the *embolon*, which was a wooden fence that ran down the middle of the course. To go really fast, a racer needed to get on the inside, close to the *embolon*, but without crashing into it. That way they could make the quickest turns round the posts at either end.

Dust filled the arena as the chariots fought each other for first place.

The spectators rose to their feet, cheering and screaming for their favourite chariots.

The drivers yelled orders to their horses. Coaches and trainers shouted orders to the drivers, and chariot owners marched up and down, yelling orders at everyone.

Hooves beat the ground to dust
with a drumming cacophony that
mixed with the jangle of harnesses,
the rumble of wheels and the cracking
of whips.

In the midst of this spectacle,
Chloe was holding her own. But none
of the boys wanted to lose. They
barged and rammed her chariot,
trying to force her off the course.

Chloe held on and kept up with the leaders, but with each lap she seemed to slip back a bit. She didn't have as much weight on the turns as the boys, so her chariot skidded a little, losing precious moments.

Kerberos was crazy with excitement. Every time Chloe came past, he howled his appreciation, straining on the leash, almost pulling Spiro onto the track.

There were only three turns left. There was no way Chloe could make up the lost ground.

Lydia marched over to Spiro. "Let the dog go!" she ordered.

"But..." Spiro hesitated for a moment, but he knew he had to do what Lydia said.

As Chloe tore past them again, Kerberos jumped onto the track. Racing after her, he leaped into the chariot and took up his position from the night before.

With each turn, Chloe's skill and Kerberos's extra weight allowed her to shave precious moments off her time.

She entered the final straight neck and neck with an older boy, who lashed and thrashed his horse to get more speed out of it.

Olly saw Chloe lean forward
and call gently to her tiring horse.
Whatever it was that she said, the
horse responded to her call. Finding
a last spurt of energy, it cranked up
its pace and crossed the finishing line
with its nose in the lead!

Olly and Spiro, usually enemies, hugged each other, dancing up and down and singing at the top of their voices. "We did it! We did it!"

Chloe slowed the chariot, turned it around and drove over to the boys. She hugged Kerberos and reached over to pat the horse's flank. "*We* did it, actually!" she panted.

Lydia turned to Chloe and the boys. She smiled coldly. "I think you'll find that *I* did it, actually!"

"But…" Olly began.

Lydia turned on her heel, waved graciously to the crowd, and marched purposefully across the track to receive her prize on the winner's podium.

Olly watched Lydia closely. She
stood tall and confident, like Artemis
in the dining-room paintings.

"I want to be just like her when
I grow up," Chloe sighed.

Olly gave his sister a nudge. "Then
you'll have to race for the stars," he
said, smiling.

OLYMPIC FACTS!

DID YOU KNOW...?

The ancient Olympic Games began over 2,700 years ago in Olympia, in southwest Greece.

The ancient Games were held in honour of Zeus, king of the gods, and were staged every four years at Olympia.

Charioteers needed to be tall and light, so quite often they were teenagers.

Most women in Ancient Greece were not allowed to play sport, but Cynisca, from Sparta, owned the winning chariot in two Olympic games.

The ancient Olympics inspired the modern Olympic Games, which began in 1896 in Athens, Greece. Today, the modern Olympic Games are still held every four years in a different city around the world.

OLYMPIA

SHOO RAYNER

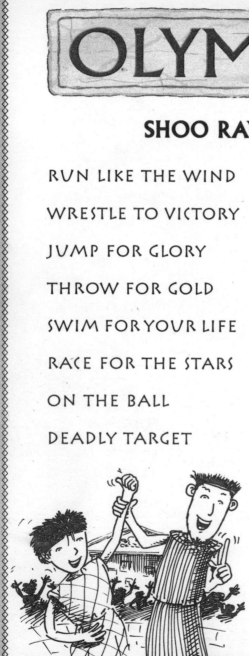